In memory of my dearest Nan, Lydia Macklin.
You're forever in our thoughts, Gatekeeper.

ISBN 978 1 78554 9496 (Paperback)
ISBN 978 1 78554 9502 (Hardback)
ISBN 978 1 78554 9519 (eBook)
www.austinmacauley.com

First Published (2016)
Austin Macauley Publishers Ltd.
25 Canada Square
Canary Wharf
London
E14 5LQ

About the Author

Joseph Hopkins is an inspiring author that writes children's stories based on personal experiences. He has two beautiful daughters, Dotty and Betty, who are often a big influence on his work. His aim is to provide fun, enjoyable and heart-warming stories to be enjoyed by families together.

To Harry James.

I hope you like
my story!

Lydia Greenfingers

was a **cute** little girl.
She had sweeping dark hair
with a touch of a **curl.**

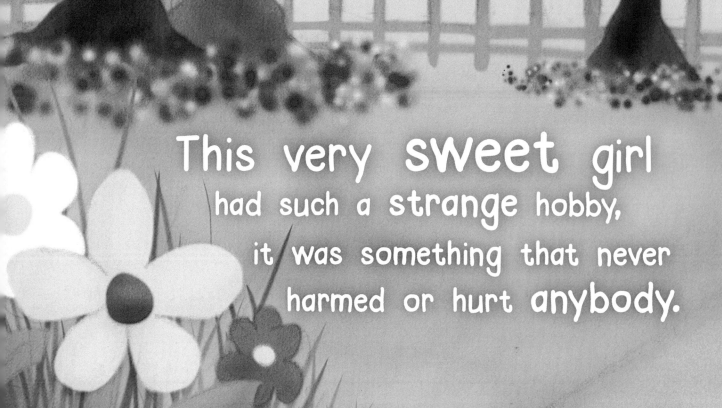

This very **sweet** girl
had such a **strange** hobby,
it was something that never
harmed or hurt **anybody.**

Lydia loved to tend to her flowers,

in the garden she'd be busy for hours and hours.

It was magical,
colourful and a sight to behold,
and all by a girl of just six years old.

For all the love Lydia had for her plants, she never felt loved by her...

strange distant aunt.

Her aunt, Synthia Slither,
had a pointy nose,
with no care or thought
for a weed or a rose.

They rarely had met
since Lydia was born,
but she was family
and Lydia was told to be warm.

Then one sad day Lydia's life hit rock bottom,
her flowers and plants would be left to go rotten.

Lydia's parents had sadly passed,
she had to leave home and her vivid green grass.

HURSELL TO

To her
HORROR
her aunt's was her destination
and their eyes met at the dingy dark station.

Her aunt shook a finger
and gestured to follow,
her eyes looked scary,
dark and hollow.

As they drove down the drive
to the dark old house,
little Lydia let out a GASP from her mouth.

The grounds were a state; the plants were all dead,

even the gnome had lost his head.

The trees were sad and their branches were bare,
how was it possible
for her aunt not to care?

Lydia felt SCARED
and she longed for her home,
but there was no one to help
or even to phone.

After three
silent
days

Aunt
Synthia
left town,
it was all in a note
that she scribbled down.

08-04-14

I'm off to work
and it's far away.
Don't make a mess –
there is food on the tray.
I'll be gone a few days,
at the most for a week.

This brought a smile
to Lydia's cheeks.

She did a little dance and she jumped about,
she let out a SCREAM and then a loud SHOUT.
This house was too dark and needed some light.
Lydia decided that she'd put things right.

She went to the shed and *pushed* open the door.
Her task then became **harder** than ever before.
Broken pots and lots of DEAD flowers,
this would take her hours and hours.

She dug,
planted and watered
until her hands were red
and after six days she stooped off to bed.
She slept like a log and she had a strange dream.
She saw both her passed parents
stood by a stream.

She woke with a fright and a slam of a door,
her aunt was back and she let out a ROAR!
"What has happened? What is wrong with my house?
Lydia get down here you daft little mouse!"

Lydia reluctantly *pushed* open the door
and dropped something accidently onto the floor.
Her aunt's furious face slightly tilted,
and she fell to her knees like her flowers when wilted.

She picked up the dropped picture into her hand,
tears swept her cheeks like the waves on the sand.
It was Lydia's mum, Synthia's sister,
oh how she wished she could hug her and kiss her.

Synthia Slither looked up at the girl,
then glanced round the room that now shone like a pearl.
She took her hand and walked Lydia outside.
"I have something to show you that I shouldn't hide."

Aunt Synthia held Lydia
and it made her face beam,
then she showed her the stream
that she'd seen in her dream.
  "This is where me and your mummy would play.
  I'm sorry I've been so sad up 'til today.

I miss your mummy so much
          and it's made my life swirl,
                but now I've got you
                like my own little girl.

I promise to make you as happy as ever,
we'll make my garden stunning together.

Your kindness and talents
are worth more than gold,
let's make this garden
a sight to behold."

Lydia Greenfingers peered into the stream,
in the reflection she saw her own little face gleam.
It was then she felt like she was in her parents' arms,
and for the first time since they left
she felt safe from all harm.

A Poem to Nan

Gatekeeper

You're now the wind that sweeps the sky
and blows through Hursell farm trees.
I feel you by my side each day
and that's what comforts me.
I've pictures 'n memories to remember you,
and your love is stuck in my heart.
I think of you each rising day that is about to start.

I approach the gate where you would sit
and wave us all away,
I now do it with a breaking heart
that lingers through my day.
I stop at work and think of you and why you had to go,
I think of all the memories of you and me, your Joe.

Returning through the gate at night I look to where you
were, and all it does is pain me deep
and cause my heart to stir.

I miss you, Gatekeeper, I love you so much
and I wish you could have stayed.
I now dread leaving and passing your gate
as I know that you've gone away.
I still look in that direction and picture you standing there,
waving to all of our family, with the wind blowing
in your white hair.

I look at the stars now, Gatekeeper, and know that you
watch over me, but I still miss you Gatekeeper,
and so do Lis, Dotts and Betty.
You've created such a close loving family,
which will keep your spirit well,
from Mum, Auntie, Rob, Little Joe
and also my big sister Kel.

I promise to look after our family
and be the best man that I can,
you've been an inspiration,
and for that I thank you, Nan.

It's time now to rest, dear Gatekeeper,
and be peaceful and comforted knowing,
we'll never forget you Gatekeeper,
now it's time for me to get going.

My last words will hopefully find you,
as you perch up there on a cloud.
I love you dearly Gatekeeper,
I just hope that I make you proud.